Inside the NFL

THE
PITTSBURGH
STEELERS

BOB ITALIA
ABDO & Daughters

Published by Abdo & Daughters, 4940 Viking Drive, Suite 622, Edina, Minnesota 55435.

Copyright © 1996 by Abdo Consulting Group, Inc., Pentagon Tower, P.O. Box 36036, Minneapolis, Minnesota 55435 USA. International copyrights reserved in all countries. No part of this book may be reproduced in any form without written permission from the publisher.

Printed in the United States.

Cover Photo credit: World Wide Photos / Allsport
Interior Photo credits: Wide World Photos, pages 4, 7, 12, 20
                              Bettmann Photos, pages 5, 6, 8,10, 11, 14, 22, 25, 29

Edited by Kal Gronvall

Italia, Bob, 1955-
        The Pittsburgh Steelers / Bob Italia.
            p. cm. -- (Inside the NFL)
Includes index.
Summary: Describes the formation, history, and key players of the football team holding an NFL record for winning the Super Bowl four times.
        ISBN 1-56239-526-2
1. Pittsburgh Steelers (Football team)--Juvenile literature. [1. Pittsburgh Steelers (Football team) 2. Football--History.] I. Title. II. Series:
Italia, Bob, 1955- Inside the NFL.
GV956.P57I82   1995
796.332'64'0974886--dc20   95-22314
                                                                          CIP
                                                                          AC

CONTENTS

One of the Greatest....................4

Art Rooney 6

The Steelers are Born 8

Buddy Parker 9

Chuck Noll 10

Terry Bradshaw 11

Franco Harris 13

The Immaculate Reception 14

Super Steelers 15

The Second Dynasty 20

The 1990s 23

Glossary 29

Index 31

One of the Greatest

The Steelers of the 1970s were one of the greatest teams in professional football history. Their four Super Bowl wins set an NFL record. The defensive "Steel Curtain" of "Mean" Joe Greene, Dwight "Mad Dog" White, Ernie Holmes, and L.C. Greenwood dominated the NFL. Quarterback Terry Bradshaw, running back Franco Harris, and wide receiver Lynn Swann formed a potent offense.

The Steelers of the 1990s mirror that great 1970s team. Rod Woodson and Kevin Greene anchor one of the NFL's top-rated defenses. Quarterback Neil O'Donnell spearheads a potent offense. All that is lacking is a Super Bowl championship—something they nearly accomplished in 1994. Once the trophy is seized, Pittsburgh may well be on their way to another football dynasty.

Terry Bradshaw led the Steelers offense for many years.

Lynn Swann was part of the Steelers' potent offense.

Art Rooney

For many years, the Pittsburgh Steelers had a losing tradition. The team had mediocre coaching and few star players. Talk of championships never crept into the Pittsburgh locker room. But owner Art Rooney was a patient man, and never gave up on his team.

Born in 1901, Arthur Joseph Rooney was the eldest of nine children. Art's father, Daniel, owned a saloon a few blocks from Exposition Park where baseball's Pittsburgh Pirates played their games. (Today, it is the site of Three Rivers Stadium.) As a boy, Rooney loved to play football and baseball. Rooney and his friends watched Pirates games through the knotholes in the wooden fence surrounding Exposition Park. Like most boys, Rooney dreamed of one day playing professional baseball.

Years later, Rooney signed a contract to play baseball for the Boston Red Sox. But Rooney hurt his arm, ending his baseball career. He remained determined, however, to make a living in professional sports.

In 1931, Rooney formed a team for the National Football League. He called them the Pittsburgh Pirates, after his favorite baseball team. The Pirates had striped jerseys that made the players look like prisoners. Opposing teams called the Pirates "jailbirds."

The Pirates did not play well their first season. They finished with a 2-10 record. Eager for a fresh start, Rooney bought new uniforms. He also kept up his search for new talent that would turn his team into winners.

**Opposite page:
Steelers founder
Art Rooney.**

The Steelers are Born

After nine years of losing, Rooney decided, in 1940, to change his team's name to the Steelers—a nickname that reflected the city's role in building America's industrial might. Though the name sounded impressive, the new Steelers did not immediately live up to their tough billing.

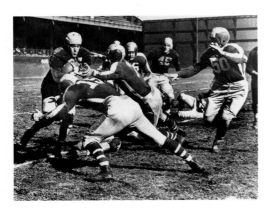

Bill Dudley carries the ball for Pittsburgh against the Eagles, 1942.

But in 1942, the Steelers finished with a 7-4 record under head coach Walt Kiesling. It was Pittsburgh's first-ever winning season. That season, running back Bill Dudley led the league in rushing. Unfortunately for Rooney, Dudley and other star players joined the army the following year to serve in World War II. Rooney's bad luck would continue for many years.

Kiesling's coaching decisions were also typical of the Steelers' luck in their early days. In 1955, Kiesling wanted to cut Johnny Unitas even though the young quarterback never played in a game. Kiesling told Rooney that Unitas could not remember the plays. "He's too dumb," the coach said to Rooney.

Rooney took Kiesling's word and released Unitas. Unitas went on to lead the Baltimore Colts to three championships and is considered one of the greatest quarterbacks in NFL history. It was these kinds of decisions that kept the Steelers on the bottom of the NFL year after year. If Pittsburgh wanted to improve, the head coach had to be more patient with the players they chose. Realizing this fact, Rooney made a head coaching change in 1957 that would lift the Steelers from the bottom of the NFL heap.

Buddy Parker

In 1957, Rooney chose Buddy Parker as his new head coach. Parker's first official act put the Steelers into high gear. He made Bobby Layne the starting quarterback—and almost immediately, Pittsburgh began to win. Parker also had Hall of Fame running back John Henry Johnson. Johnson was known for running over bold defensive players who tried to tackle him. On defense, Gene "Big Daddy" Lipscomb destroyed the opponent's offensive scheme.

Bobby Layne.

With Buddy Parker's leadership, the Steelers had five non-losing records in eight years. In 1962, Pittsburgh finished 9-5 to make the playoffs. Their championship hopes ended with a 17-10 loss to Detroit.

Parker led the Steelers to another winning record in 1963. But in 1964, the Steelers fell to 5-9. Rooney made another coaching change, hiring Mike Nixon for the 1965 season. But things got worse as Pittsburgh won only two games. Bill Austin took over in 1966, but the Steelers only improved slightly to 5-8-1. The following season, Pittsburgh finished 4-9-1. And in 1968, Austin's team hit rockbottom with a 2-11-1 campaign.

When the disaster was through, so was Austin. Having once again witnessed his beloved team fall into a losing tradition, Rooney searched for a head coach who would keep the Steelers, at the very least, a competitive team—and perhaps even win an NFL championship. To fill the job, Rooney looked to the Baltimore Colts and their assistant coach, Chuck Noll.

9

Chuck Noll

In 1969, Charles Henry "Chuck" Noll became the Steelers fourteenth head coach. In just a few short years, Noll would build Pittsburgh's perennial losers into one of the NFL's greatest dynasties.

Noll was the patient head coach Rooney had been searching for since the Steelers were born. He carefully selected talent from the college draft to build the team rather than trading for veterans. Most importantly, Noll knew what it took to win an NFL championship: defense.

In 1969, Noll used his number-one draft pick to select Joe Greene from North Texas State. Greene was a ferocious defensive tackle—the first of the most successful line of draft selections in NFL history. Noll also added offensive lineman Jon Kolb from Oklahoma State and linebacker L.C. Greenwood from Arkansas AM & N.

Greene turned out to be as ferocious as Noll had hoped. Though his team won only one game that season, Noll remained patient—and looked forward to another successful college draft in 1970.

The Steelers and the Bears had tied for the worst record in the NFL. To decide which team would receive the first pick in the college draft, NFL commissioner Pete Rozelle held a coin toss in New Orleans. The Steelers called "heads." As the coin settled on the floor, Rozelle announced that the coin had, indeed, come up heads. Pittsburgh had the first pick in the college draft. The Steelers left little doubt about who they wanted. He was the nation's best college quarterback: Louisiana Tech's Terry Bradshaw.

Terry Bradshaw

Terry Bradshaw was born September 2, 1948, in Shreveport, Louisiana. Bradshaw began playing football at an early age. But many coaches thought he was too skinny. In junior high school, Bradshaw was cut from the team. He was so upset, he cried when he got home from practice. But his father knew that Bradshaw was still growing. "You're time will come," he told his son. "Just make sure that you're ready when it does."

Bradshaw did not give up. By the time he was a senior in high school, he became the starting quarterback. Bradshaw completed 47 percent of his passes for 1,400 yards and 21 touchdowns. Over 200 colleges around the country offered him scholarships—not because of his ability to throw a football, but rather, his ability to throw the javelin.

Pittsburgh quarterback, Terry Bradshaw.

Bradshaw joined the track team so he could have a spring sport. His arm got so strong from throwing the javelin that by twelfth grade, he was the best high school javelin thrower in the country. Bradshaw set the national high school record of 244 feet 11 inches. Bradshaw turned all the track scholarships down because he wanted to play college football.

Terry Bradshaw hands off the ball to Franco Harris.

Louisiana State was one of the few schools that offered Bradshaw a football scholarship. Since Bradshaw wanted to play as a freshman, he chose Louisiana Tech, a small college only 75 miles from his home. By the time he graduated, Bradshaw was a muscular six-foot three-inch, 215-pound man. Even more, Bradshaw was quick. He could run the 40-yard dash in 4.6 seconds.

Bradshaw's first game as a Steeler was not a memorable one. In one stretch, he threw nine-straight incompletions. His passes often wobbled. A few were intercepted. After going 4-for-16, Noll finally benched him. He would struggle throughout the season.

One day, Bradshaw's old college coach sent him films from Bradshaw's college games. The young quarterback studied the films and rediscovered what made him successful. More importantly, he saw that he was a good quarterback. His confidence grew.

Meanwhile, Noll continued drafting bigger, faster, and better players. In 1970 and 1971, he signed Mel Blount, Frank Lewis, John McKin, and Joe Gilliam. Slowly, Noll was building a championship team. But he still needed a quality running back.

Franco Harris

Noll found his running back at Penn State University. There, Franco Harris was shredding opponents' defenses.

Harris was the key ingredient to the Steelers' success. Each year, they were getting better and better. All they needed was the catalyst— and Harris was it.

But in 1972, Harris got off to a slow start. In his first game, Harris rushed for only 35 yards and fumbled twice in a loss to Cincinnati. Backfield coach Dick Hoak thought he had a real dud on his hands.

But halfway through his rookie season, Harris found his stride. He rushed for over 100 yards in six straight games, equaling Jim Brown's NFL record. With Harris running wild, the Steelers won nine of their next ten games and gained a playoff berth for the first time since 1962.

Franco Harris was the key to the Steelers offense.

The Immaculate Reception

In Pittsburgh's first playoff game, the Steelers faced the Oakland Raiders. In a defensive battle at Pittsburgh, the Steelers trailed 7-6 with only 22 seconds remaining. Bradshaw had one play left. He called, "66 option." In the Raiders defensive huddle, defensive back Jack Tatum—the man they called "the Assassin"— glared at the Steelers and grumbled, "One more time."

From his own 40-yard line, Bradshaw took the snap, rolled to his right, and threw to running back John Fuqua. Just as the ball arrived, Tatum collided violently with Fuqua, and the ball flew 15 yards backward to Harris, who was following the play.

As the ball fell toward the ground, Harris reached down and plucked the ball off his shoe tops. Tucking the ball under his arm, he rambled 60 yards and avoided one last Oakland defender to score the winning touchdown. The stadium erupted in celebration. Harris' "Immaculate Reception" was one of the most dramatic plays in the history of the NFL playoffs.

In the AFC championship game, the Steelers faced the undefeated Miami Dolphins. Pittsburgh played Miami tough throughout the game, which was tied 7-7 at halftime. But the Dolphins jumped out on top in the third quarter with a touchdown and never trailed the rest of the way. A Bradshaw touchdown pass in the fourth quarter brought the Steelers within 21-17, but Pittsburgh had finally run out of magic. Next year would be a different story.

Super Steelers

The Steelers expected to reach the Super Bowl in 1973. But injuries to Harris and Bradshaw derailed those plans. The Steelers finished second to the Cincinnati Bengals, but still made the playoffs as a wildcard team. In the first round, however, the Raiders got revenge for the Immaculate Reception by destroying the Steelers 33-14.

Despite the loss, the Steelers' defense was getting stronger. Greene, Greenwood, Andy Russell, Jack Ham, and Mike Wagner all were candidates for All-Pro honors.

In 1974, Noll had his best draft ever. In five rounds, he selected Lynn Swann, Jack Lambert, John Stallworth, and Mike Webster. These players would eventually combine for 24 Pro Bowl appearances.

Joe Gilliam won the starting quarterback job. But Bradshaw earned it back in midseason. Pittsburgh then rambled through the rest of the schedule and finished in first place with a 10-3-1 record. The biggest surprise was halfback Rocky Bleier, who had recovered from leg injuries suffered in the Vietnam war to earn a starting job in the backfield.

In the first playoff game, Pittsburgh had little trouble with Buffalo as they stormed to a 29-7 halftime lead and cruised to a 32-14 win. But in the AFC title game, they would have to face the Oakland Raiders.

The score was tied 3-3 at halftime, but the Raiders seized control in the third quarter with a touchdown while keeping the Steelers scoreless. In the fourth quarter, however, Pittsburgh exploded. Harris scored on a 7-yard run and Swann followed with a 6-yard touchdown pass from Bradshaw. George Blanda kicked a 24-yard field goal for the Raiders to make the score 17-13. But Harris' 21-yard touchdown run sealed the 24-13 victory.

Suddenly, the Steelers found themselves in their first-ever Super Bowl. It took them 42 years to get to the championship game. They were not about to lose.

The Steelers faced the Minnesota Vikings and their scrambling quarterback Fran Tarkenton. The Pittsburgh defense was rock-solid the entire game and kept Tarkenton in check. Even more, they accounted for the only scoring in the first half, a 2-point safety.

The Steelers scored the game's first touchdown in the third quarter on a Harris 12-yard run. The Steelers seemed to have the game in hand in the fourth quarter when the Vikings suddenly scored after blocking a Pittsburgh punt and falling on the ball in the end zone. But the Vikings missed the extra point and trailed 9-6.

That's when Pittsburgh regained control. The Steelers went on a 65-yard drive that featured Franco Harris' strong running. It finally ended when Bradshaw hit Larry Brown in the end zone with a 4-yard pass to ice the game, 16-6. Harris set a Super Bowl record with 158 yards rushing. But no one was more excited than Art Rooney.

"Today's win made all the other years worth it," Rooney said after the game. "I am happy for the coaches and players, but I'm especially happy for the Pittsburgh fans. They deserved this."

The Steelers were not satisfied with one championship. They were young and had the potential for greatness. So they dedicated the following season to repeat. "Two for two" became their battle cry.

The Steelers were up against great odds. Only two teams had ever won back-to-back championships—the Green Bay Packers and the Miami Dolphins.

But during the 1975 season, the Steelers looked unbeatable. They won 11 consecutive games and finished 12-2. In the playoffs, they manhandled Baltimore 28-10 and defeated Oakland 16-10. Pittsburgh had defied the odds. Once again, they were headed for the Super Bowl.

This time, they faced the Dallas Cowboys. Dallas grabbed a 10-7 halftime lead and held the Steelers scoreless in the third quarter. But then Bradshaw and Swann went to work in the fourth quarter. After a Pittsburgh safety and field goal, Bradshaw hit Swann on a 64-yard scoring strike to put the Steelers up 21-10. Dallas finally countered with a touchdown of their own, but the Steelers held firm the rest of the way for a 21-17 win.

For the game, Swann caught four passes for an amazing 166 yards and a 40.3 yards-per-catch average. His efforts earned him the game's Most Valuable Player honors. With the victory, Chuck Noll joined Vince Lombardi and Don Shula as the only coaches to win consecutive Super Bowls.

Lynn Swann (88) goes up for a pass against the Raiders.

In 1976, the Steelers went for an unprecedented third Super Bowl victory in a row. After a 1-4 start, the Steelers rallied around their defense to win their last nine games and their third division title in as many years. The Steel Curtain recorded five shutouts in the last eight games. Harris and Bleier both rushed for over 1,000 yards.

In the playoffs, Pittsburgh destroyed Baltimore 40-14 and seemed on their way to the Super Bowl. But their old nemesis, the Oakland Raiders, ambushed the Steelers 24-7 in the AFC championship game.

In 1977, the Steelers finally showed signs of weakness. They started out at 4-4 and earned their fourth-straight division title on the last day of the season, finishing 9-5. In the playoffs, Denver scored at will against the once-mighty Steel Curtain and won easily 34-21. The dynasty was finally over—or was it?

PITTSBURGH STEELERS

10   20   40

Bobby Layne becomes quarterback in 1957.

Art Rooney formed the Pittsburgh football team in 1931.

PITTS
STEE

Bill Dudley leads the league in rushing in 1942.

10   20   30   40

40   20   10

Terry Bradshaw was the
number one draft pick
for the team in 1970.

URGH
LERS

Franco Harris joins
the team in 1972.

PITTSBURGH
STEELERS

40   30   20

Neil O'Donnell breaks Steelers
passing records in 1993.

The Second Dynasty

In 1978, the Steelers focused on the pass and opened up their offense. The result was amazing as the Steelers finished with a 14-2 record, the best in the NFL. The Steel Curtain was back, allowing the fewest points in the NFL. Bradshaw was also rejuvenated. He silenced his critics by leading the league in touchdown passes.

In the playoffs, Pittsburgh destroyed Denver 33-10. Then in the AFC Championship, they tore apart the Houston Oilers 34-5. Going into their third Super Bowl, the Steelers looked invincible. But they were facing the defending Super Bowl champion Dallas Cowboys.

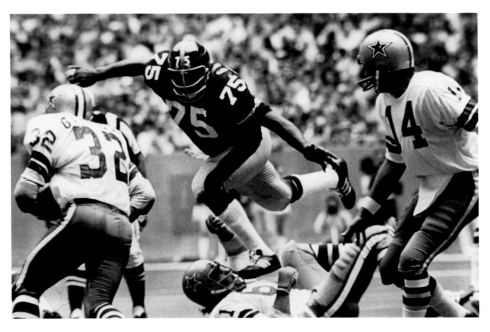

"Mean" Joe Greene (75) steps on Blaine Nye to make a tackle on a Cowboys running back.

Bradshaw played the best game of his life. He passed for 318 yards and four touchdowns, and became the first quarterback ever to win three Super Bowls.

One year later, the Steelers won their division, then pounded their way to a fourth Super Bowl appearance. The Steelers were heavily favored over the Los Angeles Rams, but the game was anything but easy.

Trailing 19-17 in the fourth quarter, the Steelers had the ball on their own 27-yard line. Bradshaw decided to go for the victory. He threw a long pass to John Stallworth. Stallworth made the catch, and dashed 73 yards for the score. The Steelers went up 24-19.

A few minutes later, Bradshaw threw a 45-yard bomb to Stallworth that set up a 1-yard touchdown run by Harris. The Steelers went on to win 31-19 and made football history with their fourth Super Bowl championship.

As the 1980s progressed, Pittsburgh slowly lost their great players to retirement. Noll tried to use the college draft once again to rebuild his team, and the Steelers strung together three more winning seasons. In 1984, the Steelers won the Central Division title for the ninth time in 13 seasons.

In the playoffs, the new Steelers—led by quarterback Mark Malone and receiver Louis Lipps—beat the Broncos, then faced the Dolphins in the AFC championship game. The Steelers, however, came up short, 45-28.

Noll's luck in the draft did not continue. He found it impossible to replace the likes of Terry Bradshaw and Joe Greene. In the next three seasons, Pittsburgh fell on hard times. By 1988, fans called for coach Noll's dismissal.

But Rooney knew that the team needed a top-notch quarterback to lead the Steelers back to the playoffs. The Steelers decided that their

quarterback of the future was Bubby Brister. Pittsburgh had drafted
him in the third round in 1986, but it took Brister a few years to work
his way into a starting position.

In 1988, Brister got his chance. His fiery leadership was the
highlight of a disappointing 5-11 campaign. Brister passed for 2,634
yards and 11 touchdowns. But he also threw 14 interceptions. The
defense could not muster much of a pass rush, and the young
secondary was picked apart. Clearly, Noll had much more rebuilding
to do.

The 1989 season started out horribly. The Steelers lost their first
two games by a combined score of 92-10. Suddenly, they were the
joke of the NFL.

But just as quickly, Pittsburgh turned their season around. With a
team that was one-fourth rookies, the Steelers roared through the
remainder of their schedule and won five of their last six games to
make the playoffs. Brister did not have great passing numbers, but he
was still the team leader. And Louis Lipps had another fine year.

In the first round of the playoffs, the Steelers surprised the Oilers
in Houston with a dramatic 26-23 overtime win. Running back Merril
Hoge tied the game in the fourth quarter with a 2-yard run, and Gary
Anderson won it with a 50-yard field goal.

Pittsburgh nearly pulled off another upset in the second round
against the Broncos in Denver. But Denver pulled the game out late
in the fourth quarter with a touchdown that sealed a 24-23 win.
Despite the loss, Brister and company finally looked as though they
were turning things around.

The 1990s

In the 1990 season, Joe Walton was hired as offensive coordinator to redesign the offense. But the system was so complex that the Steelers did not score an offensive touchdown until the fourth game. Once the system was simplified, the Steelers began to win. A victory in the final game would have given Pittsburgh the division title. But a loss put them at 9-7 and in third place—and out of the playoffs.

Brister was erratic in 1990, but still had his best season, throwing 20 touchdown passes. Eric Green set a Steelers record for tight ends with seven touchdown catches. But the team had to rely on its defense to win. The new steel curtain allowed the fewest yards in the NFL. The secondary, led by Rod Woodson, was the NFL's best. Part of the championship puzzle was in place. Could the Steelers build a consistent offense to lead them to the Super Bowl?

The 1991 season ended up as Chuck Noll's most disappointing. The Steelers expected to make the playoffs, but were out of contention by midseason as they failed to beat winning teams for the third straight season.

The biggest shock was the fall of the defense. The offense was still sputtering. Neil O'Donnell was challenging Bubby Brister for the starting job. Tight end Eric Green was the best offensive weapon. But he was injured in Game 9.

Rod Woodson.

After the Steelers finished with a 7-9 record, Chuck Noll announced his retirement. At the time, he was the only coach to win four Super Bowls. Noll was replaced by Kansas City defensive coordinator Bill Cowher.

Cowher, only 35 years old, infused the Steelers with new enthusiasm. The Steelers responded by winning their first division title since 1984. It was also the Steelers first 11-win season since 1979 when they last won the Super Bowl.

Barry Foster was the story of the year. He led the conference in rushing with 1,690 yards and 11 touchdowns. Besides breaking many of Franco Harris' team records, he tied Eric Dickerson's league record with 12 100-yard games in a season.

O'Donnell was 9-3 as a starter before going out with a broken leg. Woodson was his usual All-Pro self. Wide receiver Jeff Graham and rookie safety Darren Perry also played well. The only dark spot was Eric Green. He had his troubles and was suspended by the league for substance abuse.

The Steelers seemed ready to march to the Super Bowl. But in the second round, they were outplayed at home by the Buffalo Bills and lost 24-3. The offense, which looked like it was getting better, reverted to its old inconsistent play, casting some doubt on the 1993 season.

The following year, the Steelers finished at 9-7 and again made the playoffs. But mistakes by the NFL's worst special teams cost the Steelers at least two victories. Foster suffered a season-ending ankle injury in the ninth game after rushing for 711 yards and scoring eight touchdowns.

With Foster gone, the Steelers scored only eight touchdowns in the final seven games. Green caught 63 passes for 942 yards, but the wide receivers dropped too many balls. O'Donnell struggled with tendinitis in his throwing elbow but still broke Bradshaw's team record for attempts and completions.

Neil O'Donnell throws a
pass against the Cleveland
Browns, 1995.

In the playoffs against Kansas City, Pittsburgh jumped out to a 17-7 halftime lead against the Chiefs. But late in the fourth quarter, Kansas City tied the game 24-24 with a touchdown, sending the contest into overtime. The Chiefs got the ball and drove down the field, setting up a game-winning 32-yard field goal.

Pittsburgh was in a dilemma. Their team was good enough to consistently make the playoffs, but they couldn't go anywhere after that. The missing ingredient seemed to be with the offense—but what? If they could only play consistently.

The Steelers began the 1994 season with a 26-9 loss to the World Champion Dallas Cowboys. Halfway through the season, they were 5-2 and in second place—one game behind the first-place Cleveland Browns. By Week 11, their record had ballooned to 7-3. But they were still trailing the Browns by one game.

The breakthrough came in Week 12 with a 16-13 overtime win against Miami as Gary Anderson kicked a 39-yard field goal with 4:41 left. It was Anderson's third field goal of the game and nineteenth in a row. Mike Tomczak, who replaced injured Neil O'Donnell, passed for 343 yards and directed the 66-yard overtime drive that set up Anderson's game-winning kick.

The Steelers seized control of first place in Week 14 by breezing past the Bengals 38-15. In doing so, the Steelers wrapped up a playoff spot, although they were hoping for more. "We want home-field-advantage," Woodson said. "It will be very hard for teams to come into Pittsburgh and win."

For the last two months, it had been very hard for opponents to beat the Steelers anywhere. Pittsburgh's win over Cincinnati was their fifth in a row and eight in nine games.

The defense was the big story. The Steelers sacked Bengals quarterback Jeff Blake 5 times, increasing their total to an NFL-leading 50.

On offense, rookie Bam Morris rushed for 108 yards and 2 touchdowns, while O'Donnell threw a pair of touchdowns.

In Week 16, Pittsburgh faced a division showdown with second-place Cleveland. A victory would wrap up the division for the Steelers.

A record crowd of 60,808 cheered the Steelers to a 17-7 victory as they won their seventh game in a row. They seized a 14-0 lead with touchdowns on their first two possessions. O'Donnell fired a 40-yard scoring pass to Yancey Thigpen, then hit Ernie Mills with a 42-yard pass that set up a Foster 1-yard touchdown run. Foster, who played with two cracked vertebrae in his lower back, carried 32 times for 106 yards.

Quarterback Neil O'Donnell celebrates a touchdown.

"This is a championship-caliber team," lineman Kevin Greene said. "We proved it tonight."

Though Pittsburgh stumbled 37-34 to San Diego in the final week, they clinched home-field advantage for the playoffs with their AFC-best 12-4 record. Now the playoffs loomed ahead.

Cleveland was the second-round opponent. The two teams had played a pair of close, hard-fought games earlier in the season, both won by Pittsburgh.

The Steelers won more easily this time. Playing at home, they scored on their first three drives for a 17-0 lead. They stretched it to 24-3 at halftime and put Cleveland away 29-9.

In all, the Steelers outgained the Browns 424-186. They rushed for 238 yards, including 133 by Foster and 60 by Morris. Their victory sent them to the AFC title game for the first time since 1984. Their opponent? The San Diego Chargers.

The Chargers had lost six games in a row and nine of ten overall at Pittsburgh's Riverfront Stadium. They trailed the Steelers 13-3 in the third quarter and seemed destined for another defeat. But San Diego rallied to take a 22-21 lead late in the fourth quarter.

That's when O'Donnell took over. Pittsburgh took the ball on its 17 and surged 80 yards as O'Donnell completed his first 7 passes on the drive and 8 of his first 9.

But at the San Diego three, with 1:04 left, the Chargers knocked down O'Donnell's fourth-down pass intended for Foster in the end zone. The shocked Steelers, who had won eight consecutive games at home, were out of the playoffs.

For the day, O'Donnell passed for 349 yards, setting AFC title game records with 32 completions and 54 attempts. But he would have traded it all in for a win and a chance at a Super Bowl title.

Despite the loss, the Steelers finally seemed to be on the brink of another championship team. The defense has established itself as one of the NFL's best. If the offense can play consistently in the years to come, look for Pittsburgh to claim its record-tying fifth Super Bowl title.

GLOSSARY

ALL-PRO—A player who is voted to the Pro Bowl.

BACKFIELD—Players whose position is behind the line of scrimmage.

CORNERBACK—Either of two defensive halfbacks stationed a short distance behind the linebackers and relatively near the sidelines.

DEFENSIVE END—A defensive player who plays on the end of the line and often next to the defensive tackle.

DEFENSIVE TACKLE—A defensive player who plays on the line and between the guard and end.

ELIGIBLE—A player who is qualified to be voted into the Hall of Fame.

END ZONE—The area on either end of a football field where players score touchdowns.

EXTRA POINT—The additional one-point score added after a player makes a touchdown. Teams earn extra points if the placekicker kicks the ball through the uprights of the goalpost, or if an offensive player crosses the goal line with the football before being tackled.

FIELD GOAL—A three-point score awarded when a placekicker kicks the ball through the uprights of the goalpost.

FULLBACK—An offensive player who often lines up farthest behind the front line.

FUMBLE—When a player loses control of the football.

GUARD—An offensive lineman who plays between the tackles and center.

GROUND GAME—The running game.

HALFBACK—An offensive player whose position is behind the line of scrimmage.

HALFTIME—The time period between the second and third quarters of a football game.

INTERCEPTION—When a defensive player catches a pass from an offensive player.

KICK RETURNER—An offensive player who returns kickoffs.

LINEBACKER—A defensive player whose position is behind the line of scrimmage.

LINEMAN—An offensive or defensive player who plays on the line of scrimmage.

PASS—To throw the ball.

PASS RECEIVER—An offensive player who runs pass routes and catches passes.

PLACEKICKER—An offensive player who kicks extra points and field goals. The placekicker also kicks the ball from a tee to the opponent after his team has scored.

PLAYOFFS—The postseason games played amongst the division winners and wild card teams which determines the Super Bowl champion.

PRO BOWL—The postseason All-Star game which showcases the NFL's best players.

PUNT—To kick the ball to the opponent.

QUARTER—One of four 15-minute time periods that makes up a football game.

QUARTERBACK—The backfield player who usually calls the signals for the plays.

REGULAR SEASON—The games played after the preseason and before the playoffs.

ROOKIE—A first-year player.

RUNNING BACK—A backfield player who usually runs with the ball.

RUSH—To run with the football.

SACK—To tackle the quarterback behind the line of scrimmage.

SAFETY—A defensive back who plays behind the linemen and linebackers. Also, two points awarded for tackling an offensive player in his own end zone when he's carrying the ball.

SPECIAL TEAMS—Squads of football players that perform special tasks (for example, kickoff team and punt-return team).

SPONSOR—A person or company that finances a football team.

SUPER BOWL—The NFL Championship game played between the AFC champion and the NFC champion.

T FORMATION—An offensive formation in which the fullback lines up behind the center and quarterback with one halfback stationed on each side of the fullback.

TACKLE—An offensive or defensive lineman who plays between the ends and the guards.

TAILBACK—The offensive back farthest from the line of scrimmage.

TIGHT END—An offensive lineman who is stationed next to the tackles, and who usually blocks or catches passes.

TOUCHDOWN—When one team crosses the goal line of the other team's end zone. A touchdown is worth six points.

TURNOVER—To turn the ball over to an opponent either by a fumble, an interception, or on downs.

UNDERDOG—The team that is picked to lose the game.

WIDE RECEIVER—An offensive player who is stationed relatively close to the sidelines and who usually catches passes.

WILD CARD—A team that makes the playoffs without winning its division.

ZONE PASS DEFENSE—A pass defense method where defensive backs defend a certain area of the playing field rather than individual pass receivers.

INDEX

A

Anderson, Gary 22, 26
Arkansas AM & N 10
Austin, Bill 9

B

Blake, Jeff 26
Blanda, George 15
Blount, Mel 12
Bradshaw, Terry 4, 10-12, 14-17,
    20, 21
Brister, Bubby 21-23
Brown, Jim 13
Brown, Larry 16

C

Cowher, Bill 24

D

Dallas Cowboys 17, 26
defense 4, 9, 23, 26, 28
Dickerson, Eric 24
Dudley, Bill 8

E

Exposition Park 6

F

Foster, Barry 24, 27, 28
Fuqua, John 14

G

Gilliam, Joe 12, 15
Graham, Jeff 24
Green Bay Packers 16
Green, Eric 23, 24
Greene, "Mean" Joe 4, 10, 15,
    21
Greene, Kevin 4, 27
Greenwood, L.C. 4, 10, 15

H

Ham, Jack 15
Harris, Franco 4, 13, 14, 15, 16,
    17, 21
Hoak, Dick 13
Holmes, Ernie 4

J

javelin 11
Johnson, John Henry 9

K

Kiesling, Walt 8
Kolb, Jon 10

L

Lambert, Jack 15
Lewis, Frank 12
Lipps, Louis 21, 22
Lipscomb, Gene "Big Daddy" 9
Lombardi, Vince 17
Louisiana Tech 10

M

Malone, Mark 21
McKin, John 12
Miami Dolphins 16
Mills, Ernie 27
Morris, Bam 27, 28

N

NFL 4, 10, 13, 20, 23, 24, 26, 28
Nixon, Mike 9
Noll, Chuck 9, 10, 12, 13, 15, 17,
    21, 22, 24
North Texas State 10

O

Oakland Raiders 14
O'Donnell, Neil 4, 23, 24, 26,
    27, 28
offense 4, 23, 24, 26, 27
Oklahoma State 10

P

Parker, Buddy 9
Penn State University 13
Perry, Darren 24
Pittsburgh Pirates 6
Pro Bowl 15

R

Rooney, Art 6, 8, 9, 10, 16, 21
Rooney, Daniel 6
Rozelle, Pete 10
Russell, Andy 15

S

Shreveport, Louisiana 11
Shula, Don 17
Stallworth, John 15, 21
"Steel Curtain" 4, 23
Super Bowl 4, 16, 17, 21, 23, 24,
    28
Swann, Lynn 4, 15, 17

T

Tarkenton, Fran 16
Tatum, Jack 14
"Immaculate Reception, The" 14
Thigpen, Yancey 27
Three Rivers Stadium 6
Tomczak, Mike 26

U

Unitas, Johnny 8

W

Wagner, Mike 15
Walton, Joe 23
Webster, Mike 15
White, Dwight 4
Woodson, Rod 4, 23, 24, 26
World War II 8